JENNY'S
choice

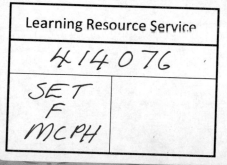

For my father,
James Edward Moore Green

Published in 2013 in Great Britain by
Barrington Stoke Ltd
18 Walker Street, Edinburgh, EH3 7LP

www.barringtonstoke.co.uk

This story was first published in a different form in
Wow! 366, Scholastic Children's Books, 2008

Text © 2008 Catherine MacPhail
Illustrations © Vladimir Stankovic

Individual ISBN 978-1-78112-300-3
Pack ISBN 978-1-78112-308-9

Not available separately

Printed in China by Leo

www.barringtonstoke.co.uk

Barrington Stoke

Catherine MacPhail

JENNY'S choice

Illustrated by Vladimir Stankovic

ACORNS growing readers

Karam was going to like his new school.
He was sure of it. He was new to this city.
New to this country. He wanted to make
friends. And everyone was so nice.

Everyone but Alex.

Alex was not nice.

On Karam's first day, Alex thumped him.

There was blood all over the playground.

"Stay away from Alex," Paul told Karam.
"He used to be nice. Then, about four years
ago, he changed. Now he is evil."

6

Every day, Alex went after Karam. If only someone could help him.

But who?

One day, Karam was walking home with blood dripping from his nose. He heard the whisper of a voice in his ear.

"Karam, I can help you."

Karam spun round.

"Who said that?" he asked.

But there was no one there. Only the cold breath of the winter wind.

Karam ran all the way home. But the voice followed him.

"Karam. Karam."

He had never been so scared.

But as Karam lay in bed that night, the voice spoke kindly to him.

"Karam, Karam," it said. "My name is Jenny and I can help you."

In Karam's dreams he asked, "How? How can you help me?"

And Jenny told him.

Karam went to school the next day with a spring in his step.

When Alex rushed over to him, Karam said, "Remember Jenny, Alex? She remembers you."

Alex's face went grey. It was clear he did remember Jenny. "Jenny ... came to you?" he asked.

Karam nodded. "She says that she is my friend now."

To Karam's surprise, Alex smiled. "I am free," he said.

Karam didn't understand.

Alex explained. "Four years ago, Jenny said she was my friend. But she's not, Karam. She makes you do bad things."

"You're lying," Karam said.

Just then, Paul came over. Karam felt a tug on his hand. All by itself, Karam's hand folded into a fist and punched Paul on the nose.

Karam tried to say he was sorry. But the words wouldn't come.

It was Alex who helped Paul to his feet.

Karam felt himself change. He was angry.
He wanted to fight. What was happening
to him?

And the winter breath of her voice blew in his ear. "For the next four years, you are mine, Karam. This is a leap year ...

and you are Jenny's Choice."

Are you NUTS about stories?

MICHAEL ROSEN

Wolfman

Illustrated by Chris Mou

Pancake Face

Georgia Byng

Illustrated by Mike Phillips

Teresa Flavin

YELLOW Rabbit

Illustrated by Rich Watso

Harry and Kate
at the
Book Museum

Sophie McKenzie

ILLUSTRATED BY MARTIN REMP

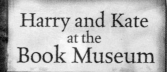

Read ALL the Acorns!